For Max, who dove right in. - DS

To my family, who have made life anything but boring...
and a special thanks to Corie and James. - DK

First paperback edition published in 2017 by Simply Read Books
First published in 2009
www.simplyreadbooks.com

Text © 2009 David Michael Slater
Illustrations © 2009 Doug Keith

Library and Archives Canada Cataloguing in Publication

Slater, David Michael, author, illustrator
        The bored book / written and illustrated by David Michael
Slater. -- First paperback edition.

Originally published: 2009.
ISBN 978-1-77229-018-9 (paperback)

        I. Title.

PZ7.S62887Bo 2016   j813'.54   C2016-901429-0

Manufactured in Korea
Original hardcover book design by Pablo Mandel / CircularStudio.com
Paperback book design by Natasha Kanji
10 9 8 7 6 5 4 3 2 1

THE BORED BOOK

David Michael Slater
Illustrations by Doug Keith

SIMPLY READ BOOKS

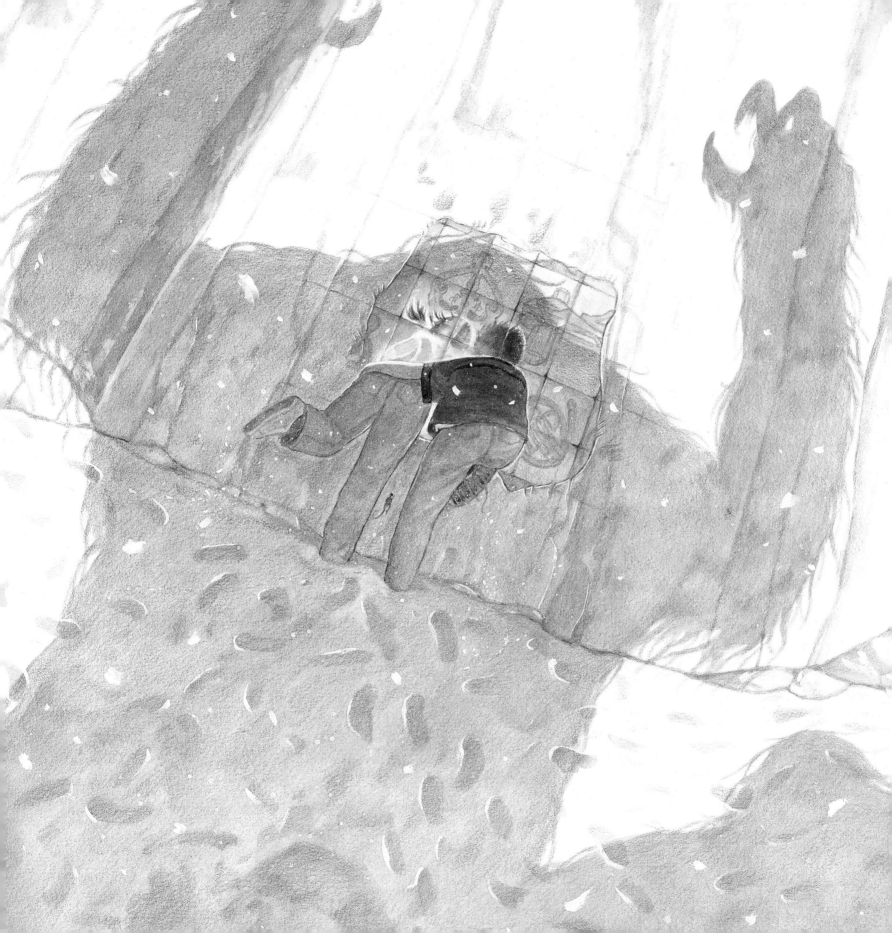